TO MUM, WHO ALWAYS TAUGHT ME TO USE THE RIGHT WORDS (I'M STILL TRYING) — J.H.

TO DAD, WHO ALWAYS WANTED ME TO BE A GUD SPELLR WITH NICE HANDWRITING :) — C.O.H.

Published in Canada and the U.S. by Kids Can Press Ltd.
25 Dockside Drive, Toronto, ON M5A 0B5

Kids Can Press is a Corus Entertainment Inc. company

www.kidscanpress.com

The artwork in this book was rendered in Photoshop.
The text is hand lettered.

Edited by Yasemin Uçar
Designed by Marie Bartholomew

Printed and bound in Shenzhen, China,
in 3/2021 by C & C Offset

CM 21 0 9 8 7 6 5 4 3 2 1

Library and Archives Canada Cataloguing in Publication

Title: Dee and Apostrofee / Judith Henderson ; [illustrated by] Ohara Hale.
Names: Henderson, Judith, author. | Hale, Ohara, illustrator.
Identifiers: Canadiana 20200373161 | ISBN 9781525303265 (hardcover)
Classification: LCC PS8615.E5225 D44 2021 | DDC jC813/.6 — dc23

Kids Can Press gratefully acknowledges that the land on which our office is located is the traditional territory of many nations, including the Mississaugas of the Credit, the Anishnabeg, the Chippewa, the Haudenosaunee and the Wendat peoples, and is now home to many diverse First Nations, Inuit and Métis peoples.

We thank the Government of Ontario, through Ontario Creates; the Ontario Arts Council; the Canada Council for the Arts; and the Government of Canada for supporting our publishing activity.

Dee and Apostrofee

Judith HENDERSON
OHARA Hale

Kids Can Press

MEET Dee.

Dee-
LIGHTED.

SHE THINKS THE BEST
WORDS START WITH HER—
the LETTER D.

MEET APOSTROF*ee*.

D'LIGHTED!

HE THINKS A LOT OF
HIMSELF — MOSTLY BECAUSE
HE DOES A LOT. LIKE, HE
MAKES WORDS SHORTER.

BUT HE'S SO CUTE.

WHO, ME?

I DON'T DEVOUR.

I DEVOUR!

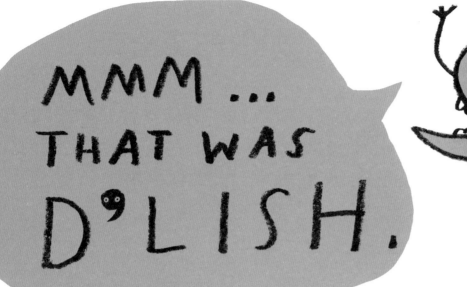

YOU SHOULD NOT!

YUM!

SHOULDN'T.

YOU COULD NOT!

COULDN'T.

YUM YUM.

APOST

A S W i

H

WHAT'S ALL the HULLABALOO?

APOSTROFee IS IN TROUBLE.

HE STOLE SO MANY O'S.

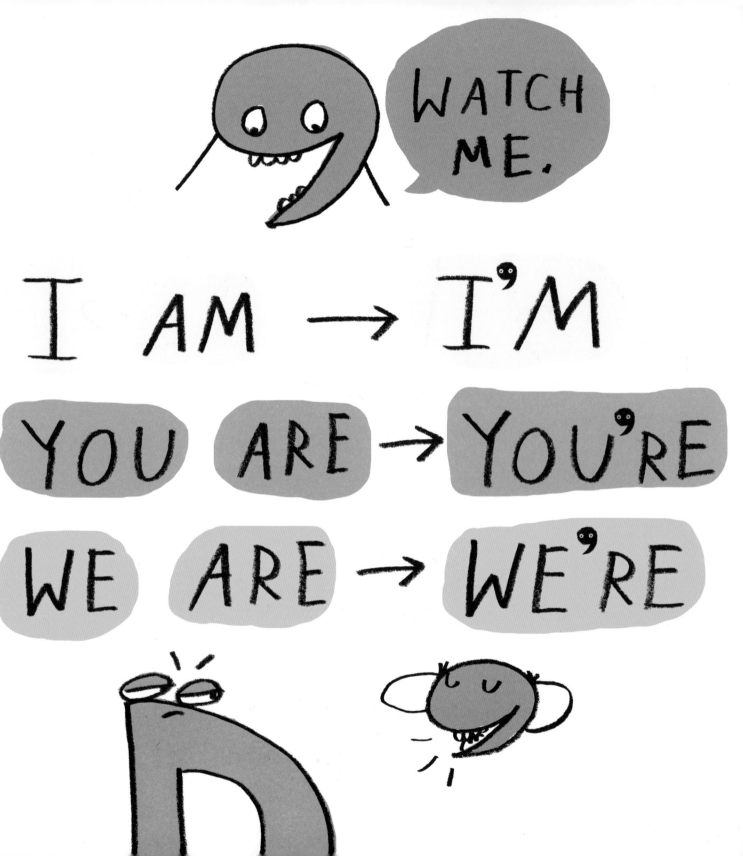

SEE? TWO WORDS COMING TOGETHER— IN PEACE 'N' HARMONY.

DOUBTFUL.

DON'T FORGET THAT WITHOUT ME YOU WOULDN'T OWN ANYTHING. I CAN GET YOU STUFF.

DO YOU MEAN STEAL?

NO! JUST POP ME IN AT THE END OF YOUR NAME, THEN ADD THE LETTER S. TRY IT! PUT YOUR NAME HERE.

This is _____'s book.

NOW the BOOK IS YOURS,

I SUPPOSE HE IS RIGHT.

S'POSE? OF COURSE I'M RIGHT!

AND YOU'RE WELCOME!

UMM ...

MAYBE WE SHOULD MAKE PEACE WITH APOSTROFEE.

OKAY, FINE'... I WILL TALK TO HIM.

HELLO, APOSTROFEE. HOW ARE YOU TODAY?

I'VE BEEN BETTER.

SHALL WE CALL A TRUCE? IF YOU STOP STEALING LETTERS, WE CAN BE ONE BIG HAPPY FAMILY!

SORRY, CAN'T.

ARE YOU SAYING YOU WILL N⊙T?

WON'T!
CAN'T!
COULDN'T!
WOULDN'T!
SHOULDN'T!
SHAN'T!

AHHHH!

BURP

UH-OH. I ATE TOO MANY ⊙'s...

THAT IS
SO SAD.

HOW WILL
HE GET
BACK?

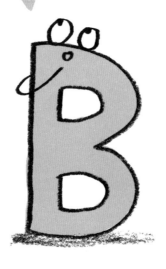

Dear
APOSTROFell,
YOU ARE
INVITED FOR
DINNER.
LET GO OF ONE
AT A TIME TO
FLOAT GENTLY DOWN.
(DO NOT EAT THEM!)
WE MISS YOU. HOPE TO
SEE YOU SOON.

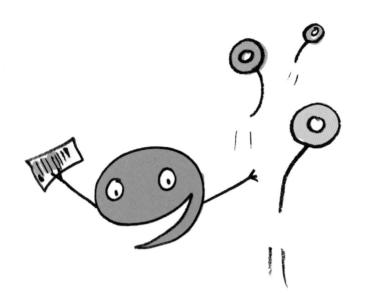

COMING IN FOR A LANDING!

DID YOU HAVE A NICE TRIP?

WELL, I WOULDN'T GO BACK.

THERE I WAS, A TINY APOSTROFee ALL ALONE IN the CLOUDS — WITH A SERIOUS CASE OF GAS, BY THE WAY.

NOBODY TOLD YOU TO EAT SO MANY O's!

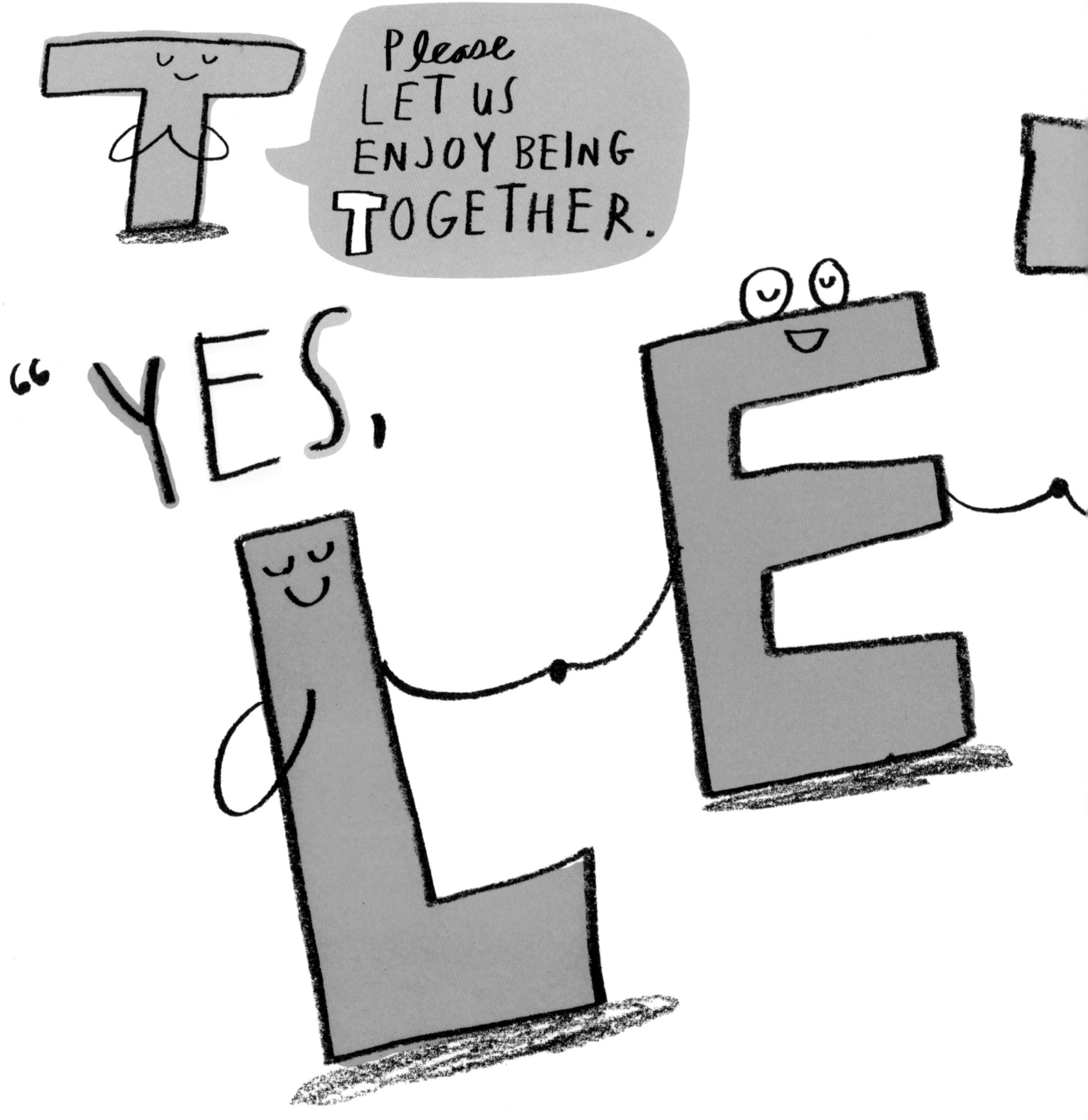
Please LET US ENJOY BEING TOGETHER.
“YES, LE